# Betrayal

## by

## Ann Jungman

## Illustrated by Alan Marks

You do not need to read this page –
just get on with the book!

First published in 2007 in Great Britain by
Barrington Stoke Ltd
18 Walker Street, Edinburgh, EH3 7LP

www.barringtonstoke.co.uk

Reprinted 2008, 2009

ISBN: 978-1-84299-466-5

Printed in Great Britain by Bell & Bain Ltd

## AUTHOR ID

**Name:** Ann Jungman

**Likes:** Quiet, good food, music, foreign films, nice people and dogs

**Dislikes:** Noise, bad manners, most fish, Britney Spears and aggression

**3 words that best describe me:**
Fat, fun and broke

**A secret not many people know:**
I was once in charge of buying chamber-pots for Her Majesty's prisons – honest!

## ILLUSTRATOR ID

**Name:** Alan Marks

**Likes:** Words, music, pictures, swimming, sunshine, people who can be bothered

**Dislikes:** Conflict, bad manners, filling out forms, exams, shopping, having my hair cut

**3 words that best describe me:**
Hard-working illustrator

**A secret not many people know:**
I got a D in A-level art

To Nicola, with love

# Contents

# Chapter 1

# A Best Friend is a Best Friend

Hannah Gluck lay in bed and listened to her parents argue. It was always the same – her mother wanted to leave Germany but her father wanted to stay.

"We have to leave, Carl, and soon. This country isn't safe for Jews any more."

"Come on, Ruth darling," Hannah's father said softly. "This Hitler can't stay in charge of Germany forever."

"Carl, how can you be so stupid!" Hannah's mother shouted. "Can't you see what's going on? You've been saying the same thing ever since that horrible little man, Hitler, came to power. Can't you see – everyone who tries to stand up to him is in prison or else they've left Germany for good. There's no one left to stand up to Hitler. He *is* here for good!"

Hannah's mother went on talking. "The only way we'll get rid of Hitler is if there's a war with another country. If we're still alive to see it happen ..." Ruth Gluck stopped talking and Hannah could hear her crying.

"Ruth, Ruth, that's rubbish," Carl Gluck said. "Why do we need to leave Germany?

Our life's not too bad and this is our home. We have a nice flat, I have a job again. The Nazis have let me work at the Jewish hospital. The children are happy in their new Jewish school. What's the big problem?"

"Carl, the Germans don't want us here. You try doing the shopping. People don't talk to me any more." Hannah's mother began to cry.

"Ruth, my dear," said Hannah's father, "it's not that easy. Where would we go?"

"We can go to England," Hannah's mother said. "We have visas and we can work there as servants. I know you hate the idea, but at least the children would be safe."

"That's crazy talk!" yelled her father. "I'm a doctor, not a servant! Now, stop this, Ruth. This is our country. I spent four years in the German army. I fought in the trenches. God knows, I have the medals to prove it. What do you think is going to happen to us here? This isn't the Middle Ages – this is Europe in 1936. Things will get better. Believe me, it'll be OK."

Hannah pulled her covers up round her ears. She wanted her father to win the argument.

*I want to stay here*, she thought. *In England we would be poor, we wouldn't have any money and we'd have to leave our flat. And I don't speak any English. And I don't want to leave Frieda. A best friend is a best friend.*

## Chapter 2
## Jews Get On Last

At breakfast the next morning, Hannah's family sat at the table tense and silent. No one said a word.

"Did you hear us arguing?" Hannah's mother asked at last.

"A bit," replied Hannah slowly.

"Well, how do you feel about it?" her mother went on. "Shall we stay or go?"

"I think Father's right," replied Hannah. "And the thought of leaving everyone and everything we know scares me to death."

"Why?" her mother asked.

"I don't speak any English and I don't have any friends there. And not all Germans hate us."

"No," agreed her mother, "but most of them do."

"Not Frieda," said Hannah. "*She* doesn't hate us!"

"But darling, her family do!" Ruth Gluck said. "Her father's in the Nazi Party now. And Frieda's mother, Mrs Wilke, doesn't talk to me any more. What's more, her brother, young Fritz, has joined the Hitler Youth. The Wilkes are Nazis and Nazis don't like Jews."

"But Frieda is different," said Hannah. "She always comes to us for Passover and I always go there for Christmas."

"You didn't go to her family last Christmas," her mother pointed out in a sad voice. "Last Christmas you were left out. Can't you see? There's no place for us here. We're not wanted. Sooner or later, even Frieda will turn her back on us."

"She won't!" shouted Hannah. "She won't, I know she won't. You're just saying that to get me to agree to go, and make Father change his mind."

"Life is so difficult," said Hannah's mother with a sigh. "And now even this family is split right down the middle. I want to go and so does your brother, but you and your father want to stay."

Hannah looked at her mother. She looked so pale and worn out that Hannah went and gave her a hug.

"It'll be alright, Mum, I know it will. It's just that Frieda and I have been best friends since ... well, since we were born. No matter how many new friends I make, no one will ever be like Frieda."

"I understand, darling. I do understand," said Hannah's mother.

"Thanks, Mum," Hannah whispered.

"Go, on," Hannah's mother went on. "You'd better get going or you'll be late for school. And if any of the Nazi bullies are outside the school, just run for your life."

As Hannah waited for the tram, she saw Frieda come out of her flat on her way to school. Frieda still went to Hannah's old school. It was the school they'd both gone to until just a few weeks ago. Now Hannah had to go to a Jewish school, which she didn't like much.

"Frieda," Hannah called out, "come and wait with me till the tram comes."

Frieda looked a bit embarrassed, and then she waved. "Sorry, I'm in a hurry," she shouted and rushed off.

As Hannah went to get onto the tram a man pushed her to one side.

"Jews get on last," he said. "Wait here until the rest of us have got on the tram."

Hannah looked up at the man and saw he had a swastika badge on the collar of his coat. She knew that the man was a member of the Nazi party. Hannah knew his face. He lived in their flats. She stood aside and let everyone else get on the tram.

On the way to school Hannah had a cold, sinking feeling.

Maybe her mother was right, maybe Germany was getting too dangerous for them. So many of their friends had left. Other Jewish families had gone to America, Australia, France and England. Some had even gone to a place called Palestine.

*Still*, Hannah thought to herself. *What Father says is true. We have been Germans for hundreds of years. We pay our taxes, we obey the laws. Father fought for Germany for four years. So did Uncle Frederick, and poor Uncle George was killed in the last*

*War. We are Germans – we are! This is our country, and that horrible Hitler can think whatever he likes.*

Outside the school there was a gang of boys. They had swastikas on their coats. They held up banners that said "Jews Out" and "Down with the Jewish scum".

Hannah ran past them and felt something soft hit her ear. She put her hand up to brush the thing away. What was it? She rubbed some gooey stuff off her neck. Someone had thrown an old tomato at her.

# Chapter 3

# Why Stay Where You're Not Wanted?

Hannah trudged up the stairs to her parents' flat after school. As she got to the second floor, she saw Frieda sitting on the stairs waiting for her.

At once Hannah felt better.

"Hi, Frieda!" she called. "Are you going to come in?"

"Just for a few minutes," agreed Frieda and she looked around quickly to make sure no one saw her going into the flat.

"What's up?" asked Hannah.

"My parents don't want me to see you any more," Frieda told her. "You know what my father and brother are like. They think that if I see you they'll get into trouble with the Nazi Party. They don't want anyone in our family mixing with Jews."

"Do you feel that way too?" asked Hannah. She felt sick thinking about it.

"No, no, of course not," Frieda answered quickly. "But I have to live with people saying terrible things about Jews every day. I know that it's not safe for your family to carry on living here. Can't you talk to your father about leaving Germany? All the other Jews I know have gone. You remember Lily and Gretel from our class? They've gone. It's the best thing to do."

"You want us to leave too?" said Hannah and her eyes filled up with tears. "You of all people, Frieda? You want to get rid of us! You're just like your father and your brother."

"No, Hannah, no – it isn't that. You will always, always be my very best and dearest friend, but I'm thinking about you and your family. Listen to me – go now, while you can. I know your mother is keen to go, and your brother Josef too. If you agree with them, your father will have to give in."

"How would you like to leave Germany?" Hannah asked. "How would you like to leave your home, your language, everything you know, and go somewhere new? Go to somewhere where you can't speak the language and don't know anyone and where you'd have no money? Would you like it?"

"No, I don't think I'd like it at all," agreed Frieda, "but if I had to go, then I would. Why do you want to stay on where you're not wanted? You can learn a new language, you can make new friends. Stop being such a coward!" And with that, Frieda walked out and slammed the door behind her.

That evening the Gluck family ate supper in silence. Hannah felt so upset that she didn't want to eat anything.

At last, Hannah's brother Josef said something. "Look, Mum, it's beginning to snow," he murmured.

They all looked out of the big dining room window, and saw that snowflakes were beginning to fall. Bit by bit a glistening layer of white was covering the city.

Hannah's father stood by the window and Hannah went and stood beside him. He put his arm round his daughter.

"Soon we'll be able to go skating," he said softly. "That'll be good, won't it?"

Hannah nodded. There were some things even the Nazis couldn't take away. Skating was one of them.

Every winter the tennis courts at the local park turned into an ice rink. The park keepers flooded the courts with water and it was so cold, the water froze at once. It was a perfect place to skate!

The snow fell for about a week. It settled for the winter. Slowly Hannah began to understand that Frieda didn't want to walk with her to the tram stop any more.

bit other people came to skate. Some of the people ignored her. A few said hello, and some gave embarrassed half smiles. Hannah just went on skating. Nothing else mattered.

After a while Frieda and her brother, Fritz, came out. He was wearing his swastika and stared hard at Hannah. He didn't say hello and Frieda skated off to the far side of the ice, far away from Hannah.

Hannah looked across and saw Kurt Brun. He was the best-looking boy at Hannah's old school and both Frieda and Hannah had always fancied him. Kurt grinned back at Hannah. Her heart gave a jump. Then she remembered she was Jewish and Kurt wasn't. She mustn't even dream about him. But, even so, she smiled back and skated on.

Hannah felt better than she had for weeks. She skated round and round, until suddenly she saw that Frieda and her brother Fritz were skating towards her at great speed.

*If they don't stop and skate around me,* Hannah thought with shock, *we'll all crash.*

But they didn't stop. They came right at her and a moment later Hannah was sprawling on the ice, legs in the air and her hat down over one eye.

Fritz began to laugh. Then, to Hannah's horror, Frieda joined in. Soon there was a group of people round Hannah, all laughing and jeering.

"Hasn't our Jewish friend got the biggest bum you ever saw?" sneered Frieda, and everyone laughed.

"Come on, Jew," shouted Fritz. "Up off that fat bum and get the hell out of here. This tennis court is a Jew-Free Zone, and don't you forget it."

Hannah just lay there in a state of shock. How could her oldest and dearest friend talk to her like that?

"Jew out, Jew out, Jew out," chanted Frieda and Fritz and they laughed louder still. Then they started to clap, and the others joined in. Hannah tried to get up but she kept slipping back down.

"If you don't get up in 30 seconds," said Frieda in a cold voice, "someone just might skate too close and take off a few of your Jewish fingers."

Everyone laughed again. Frieda skated off, and then turned and skated fast towards Hannah. Hannah had to roll over and tuck her hands under her coat. As Frieda sped past, Hannah watched her skates. They were only centimetres away from where her hands had been.

Hannah staggered to her feet. Everyone was cheering Frieda as she began to skate round and round, faster and faster.

Hannah's ankle hurt badly and her head was bleeding. She limped back to the flats. She could hear the mocking laughter behind her.

"Hannah!" she heard someone say close by. "Here – you left your hat on the ice."

She looked back. There was Kurt Brun. He held out her hat and smiled at her with kind eyes.

"Thank you, Kurt," she said. She tried hard not to let him see that she was crying.

"Come on, let me help you up to your flat," said Kurt with a smile. "It looks like you hurt your ankle pretty badly. That can be really painful. Here, take my arm."

Hannah looked into Kurt's open and friendly face. She so wanted his help. Then she thought, *He's a German too. You can't trust them. It may be a trick.*

So, with a sad smile, she said, "Thanks, Kurt, but I'll be OK on my own. Go and join your friends. It's safe out there now. It's a Jew-Free Zone."

# Chapter 5
# Time to Go

When Hannah got home, she burst into tears and couldn't stop crying. Her father bound up her ankle.

"It will hurt," he told her "but it'll get better in a few days."

"Frieda did this to me," Hannah burst out. "She did it on purpose, and then she laughed at me. I hate her. I hate her and I want to go away."

"Well, now that's three of us who want to go and you're the only one who wants to stay, Carl," said Hannah's mother. "You must agree, we must leave for England as soon as we can. No matter how difficult it is, we must go, before something really serious happens to one of the children."

"You're right," agreed Hannah's father. "I don't want to admit it, but you're right. I'll write the letter tonight. I'll write and say we'll work for that English family as their servants."

Hannah's mother gave her husband a big hug.

"It's for the best. Once we get there you can take the exams to work as a doctor in England."

A month later Hannah's family took the train out of Germany. Most of their friends had already left Germany and there was

only a very small group to wave them goodbye as the train chugged out of the station.

Hannah looked at Berlin, the city she had been born in and grown up in. As the train left the station, she thought for a split second that she saw Frieda watching the train go.

"Isn't that Frieda over there?" asked Hannah's mother.

"I doubt she'd bother to see us off," replied Hannah. "If she *is* there, it's just to make sure we go. Who cares, anyway?"

"Try not to be angry and bitter," her mother said.

"Why not? It's not as if we don't have plenty to be angry and bitter about."

"That's true," agreed her mother, "but it doesn't help. You'll make new friends in England and we'll be far away from the madness that's gripping Germany."

\*\*\*\*\*\*\*\*

Hannah's mother turned out to be right. At her new school Hannah quickly learned English and made new friends, while her parents worked as servants in the big house.

"Moving hasn't been as difficult as I thought it would be," Hannah said over dinner one night. "But I know it's been hard for you, Dad, not being able to work as a doctor."

"It has been hard," smiled Dr Gluck. "But I'm a very good butler! Better than I expected to be. And I've just had a letter to say that I can go to Edinburgh. In a year I'll be able to take my British medical exams."

"What's more," Dr Gluck went on, "I can write the exam in German. Isn't that splendid? I wouldn't be able to write in English yet. I'm not like you – you young things learn a new language so quickly!"

# Chapter 6
# At War With Germany

Hannah Gluck's family moved to Edinburgh. While their father studied to become a British doctor, Hannah and Josef had to go to another new school. They had a hard time understanding the Scottish accents of the children at their new school, but everyone was kind and helpful and very anti-Hitler.

Dr Gluck passed his exams with flying colours and then got a good job in Scotland. After Sunday lunch one day, Dr Gluck smiled at everyone round the table.

"Well, this is like the old days. I've got a good job at the hospital and a lovely home. Here I am – with my family round me and eating my wife's excellent food. What could be better?"

"Don't get too happy with life, Carl," warned Hannah's mother. "There's talk now of war with Germany."

"Will Britain really go to war with Germany?" Hannah asked her parents.

"Looks like it," replied her father. "Our dear friend Hitler's doing his best to make enemies all across Europe."

"What will happen to us?" asked Josef. "Are we British now, or are we still German?"

Ruth Gluck gave a sigh. "We're not German, but not British yet. We're refugees

– we've run away from our own country and we don't belong anywhere."

"Will you have to go and fight, Dad?" asked Hannah.

"How odd that would be," he replied. "In the last war I fought *for* Germany. In this one I might fight *against* them."

"Who will win?" Josef wanted to know. "What will happen to us if Germany wins?"

"Let's not think about that," his mother said, with a shudder.

"Oh, come on," said Hannah. "What's the worst the Nazis can do to us? I mean, they can't kill us all, can they?"

"No, of course not," said her mother quickly, "but being a Jew under Nazi rule is no picnic. Don't you remember how life was in Berlin?"

Hannah did remember. She remembered what had happened to her when she went skating that last time. She felt her legs go weak and her heart start thumping hard.

"I haven't forgotten, Mum," she muttered. "Trust me, I remember what it was like."

*******

The day Britain went to war with Germany, the Gluck family sat huddled together round their radio like every other family in Britain.

The British Prime Minister made a speech. He ended by saying, "And thus, this country is at war with Germany."

There was a terrible silence after his statement. Mrs Gluck was the first to say anything. "So what happens now?" she murmured.

"I'm going to join the army," Hannah said.

"Don't be so stupid," snapped her father. "You're too young."

"But Dad, I can't just sit here as if nothing's happening. I want to help fight Hitler."

"Finish school and then we'll talk about it," said her mother firmly. "Anyway, we don't know what's going to happen to us. The British government may arrest us and put us in prison because to them we're German. We'll just have to wait and see what they decide to do with us."

Luckily, very soon after the War started, the British government said that the Gluck family could have British passports and stay in Britain. Dr Gluck went to work in an army hospital.

Three years passed. Hannah finished school. She did join the Army, and began to work as a translator. She listened to the German radio and helped the British Army work out the German plans. As she heard about the bombing of German cities, Hannah often thought about Frieda and what her life might be like now. Even after such a long time, the horror of Frieda's betrayal made Hannah upset and scared.

*I will never forgive her, never, never,* Hannah swore to herself. *Not even if I live to be a hundred. If Frieda's been killed by a bomb, it's just what she deserves.*

# Chapter 7
# Berlin

The war went on for six years. After five years, Hannah began to see that Germany was going to lose. Britain was full of American troops waiting to fight in Europe. Hannah met David, an officer in the American army. He was keen to get married, but Hannah knew that she just didn't trust anyone any more.

"How do I know that you won't betray me, just like Frieda did?" Hannah asked David. "I just can't take that risk."

"Hey, lady, you need to do some work on yourself," David told her. "Or you're going to be one heck of a lonely girl."

When the War ended, the British Army asked Hannah to go to Germany to work as a translator there. They needed someone who could speak English and German perfectly. Hannah was keen to get away and forget about David. They'd split up when Hannah said she couldn't marry him.

"Miss Gluck, are you sure you want to go back to Germany?" asked her boss. "It's not a pretty sight, you know, and after what has happened to the Jews, you might feel very upset there."

"No," insisted Hannah. "I want to go."

When Hannah told her parents that she was going back to Germany, they were shocked.

"How can you think of going there?" her father said. "After they killed six million Jews ... Hannah, what are you thinking of?"

"I feel I need to go back to Berlin," Hannah told her parents. "I must."

"You're not just running away from here because things didn't work out with David?" asked her mother. "Such a nice boy, I don't know why you didn't marry him."

"I don't want to marry anyone!" shouted Hannah. "When you love people they can hurt you."

"That's true," agreed her mother. "But it's worth the risk, and I hope that you learn that. You must get over all that happened with Frieda. It was a long time ago – don't let it mess up your life."

*******

A few weeks later, Hannah was sitting on a train in Germany. She was on her way back to Berlin. When she looked out of the window, all she saw was ash and rubble. All the towns and villages had been bombed. When Hannah got to Berlin at last, she could hardly believe what she saw. Nearly everything had been destroyed. People were living in piles of bricks and stones. Were there any houses left?

She looked at the destruction of Berlin. This was where she'd lived when she was little. It had been a beautiful city then. Hannah felt like crying. But then she thought of Frieda. She remembered how Frieda had laughed and skated around her, how Frieda had almost cut off her fingers as Hannah lay hurt. Her heart turned to ice. *The Germans asked for it*, Hannah told herself. *They damn well asked for it.*

Hannah wanted to see the street where her family had once lived. It was very hard to find. All the bombed-out streets looked the same. At last she saw a sign on an old box. Someone had written the name of her street with some chalk. She knew this was where her family had lived.

Hannah looked up at the ruins of the block of flats. Then she saw someone creep slowly out of the cellar. It was someone she knew. With a shock Hannah saw it was Mrs Wilke, Frieda's mother. In the eight years since Hannah had left Berlin, Frieda's mother had turned into a broken old woman.

Hannah turned away, but it was too late. Frieda's mother had seen her.

"Hannah, little Hannah Gluck, is it really you?" the old lady called out.

"It is me ..." stammered Hannah. "How are you, Mrs Wilke?"

"Life has been hard on me, Hannah, very hard. Well, my white hairs tell the story. But please, come with me. I have something important to show you."

# Chapter 8
# The Truth At Last

Hannah felt a rush of panic. She wanted to run away.

"I'm very busy," she said. "I'm sorry. I need to go. I'll come and see you another time."

*Why did I come here?* Hannah thought. *I must have been crazy.*

"No, Hannah, no." Mrs Wilke said firmly. "Frieda would never forgive me if I let you go. Come now, only for ten minutes."

Mrs Wilke took Hannah by the hand and pulled her towards the cellar. Hannah was surprised at how strong the old woman's skinny hands were. She knew she could only escape if she fought with the old woman. She felt sick. She didn't want to hear about Frieda. She had no choice but to follow Mrs Wilke slowly down into the cellar where she lived.

"Did your parents and Josef survive the War?" Mrs Wilke asked.

"We all did, thank you, Mrs Wilke. And what about Mr Wilke and Fritz?" Hannah said.

"My husband was killed in an air raid. Fritz died in Russia," Mrs Wilke muttered.

"I'm sorry," said Hannah stiffly.

"You haven't asked about Frieda," Mrs Wilke went on.

"The last time I saw Frieda, she was laughing at me as I lay on the ice. My head was bleeding and it was Frieda who'd pushed me over."

"Yes," Mrs Wilke said with a sigh. "Frieda acted her part well. She took us all in."

"What do you mean?" asked Hannah.

"My daughter was never a Nazi. That was all fake. It was a cover for her real work."

"Her real work?"

"Yes. In secret, Frieda worked for a group of students who were trying to fight

Hitler. They called their group The White Rose and Frieda helped them a lot. It was no good, of course. Hitler's men found out about them and put everyone in the group to death. Frieda was shot. Some of them had their heads cut off, but Frieda was shot."

Hannah had begun to shake like a leaf. She whispered, "So why did Frieda pretend to be a Nazi?"

"To cover her tracks, of course," Mrs Wilke said. "It's all here in this diary."

"Can I read it?" asked Hannah. "Please, please let me read it!"

"Of course. That's why I wanted you to come with me."

The first thing Hannah did was look for the date when the skating accident happened. She read:

*Today I betrayed my best and dearest friend. It was the hardest thing I have ever had to do, but that idiot Hannah and her father just don't understand that they must go to England. I had to find a way to make her see that!*

*Something terrible will happen to her if they stay in Germany. Fritz was with me so it all looked real. I bet she hates me now. Kurt told me that Hannah was crying, and that made me feel awful. Kurt is such a dear. I am so glad that there is someone I can talk to, someone who understands and sees things my way.*

Tears streamed down Hannah's face.

"Oh, Mrs Wilke, I am so sorry Frieda is dead," Hannah sobbed. "She was the best friend anyone ever had. And I didn't understand what she was up to."

"I am so happy I've been able to tell you the truth about my daughter," wept Mrs Wilke. Hannah put her arms round the older woman and they cried together.

"And Kurt, what happened to Kurt?" asked Hannah as she dried her eyes.

"Kurt married Frieda and they worked together. They were happy, as much as anyone could be happy in such terrible times. Kurt died with Frieda."

"I'm so glad – so very, very glad that Frieda knew love before she died," said Hannah.

As Hannah said good-bye to Mrs Wilke she felt more peaceful than she had for a long time. Frieda was dead, but Frieda had not betrayed her.

Hannah found a flower shop and bought a big bunch of white roses. She put them outside the prison where Frieda had been shot. On the card she wrote:

*To Frieda, a good brave German and my very best friend always. She will live in my memory and the memory of my children for ever.*

That night Hannah sat up late. She wanted to write a letter to David. In the end, all she wrote was:

*Dear David,*

*I feel ready to trust. Please forgive me.*

*All my love,*

*Hannah.*

Barrington Stoke would like to thank all its readers for commenting on the manuscript before publication and in particular:

Roland Barrett
Jonathan Crawford
Madeleine Flude
Rose-Mary Gower
Kathryn Hagar
Stefan Hanegraaf
Ana South

## Become a Consultant!

Would you like to give us feedback on our titles before they are published? Contact us at the email address below – we'd love to hear from you!

info@barringtonstoke.co.uk
www.barringtonstoke.co.uk

# Also by the same author ...

# Siege!

What if your whole world was turned upside down in one day? One moment Ivan is day-dreaming in class, the next he's fighting for survival.

The German army has invaded Russia and there's only Ivan to look after his sister and baby brother.

Can they make it through the siege?

**You can order *Siege!* directly from our website at www.barringtonstoke.co.uk**